Darwin

Drako

Yellow Kitty

In memory of Nana Pauli, who admired, supported in every way,
and deeply adored her grandson, Marcus (aka Dragonboy)

About This Book

The illustrations for this book were done in acrylic paints on wood panels. This book was edited by Deirdre Jones and designed by Véronique Lefèvre Sweet. The production was supervised by Virginia Lawther, and the production editor was Annie McDonnell. The text was set in Nicolas Cochin Regular, and the display type is hand lettering.

Hachette Book Group • 1290 Avenue of the Americas, New York, NY 10104 • Visit us at LBYR.com • First Edition: September 2022 • Little, Brown and Company is a division of Hachette Book Group, Inc. • The Little, Brown name and logo are trademarks of Hachette Book Group, Inc. • The publisher is not responsible for websites (or their content) that are not owned by the publisher. • Library of Congress Cataloging-in-Publication Data • Names: Napoleoni, Fabio, author, illustrator. | Napoleoni, Fabio, illustrator. • Title: Dragonboy and the wonderful night / Fabio Napoleoni. • Description: First edition. | New York, NY : Little, Brown and Company, 2022. | Series: [Dragonboy] | Audience: Ages 4–8. | Summary: "Dragonboy and his stuffed animal friends explore the wonders of nighttime, from hooting owls to starry skies, and discover that darkness does not always have to feel scary"— Provided by publisher. • Identifiers: LCCN 2022007795 | ISBN 9780316462181 (hardcover) • Subjects: CYAC: Toys—Fiction. | Animals—Fiction. | Night—Fiction. | Fear—Fiction. | LCGFT: Picture books. • Classification: LCC PZ7.1.N363 Dt 2022 | DDC [E]—dc23 • LC record available at https://lccn.loc.gov/2022007795 • ISBN 978-0-316-46218-1 • PRINTED IN U.S.A. • PHX • 10 9 8 7 6 5 4 3 2 1

DRAGONBOY
and the Wonderful Night

Written and Illustrated by

Fabio Napoleoni

Ⓛ Ⓑ

Little, Brown and Company
New York Boston

Once upon an evening,
not too far from you,
at the very edge of the backyard,
Dragonboy was getting ready
for his next adventure.

"The night is just waking up," he said to his friends. "Let's go!"

"I wonder what's out there,"
said Yellow Kitty.
(Wondering often leads to
something wonderful.)

"Anything that isn't there in the day,
I would think," said Dragonboy.

"There's only one way to find out!" said
Drako, rushing into the shadows.

The others followed Drako, but Simon stayed put.

"I'm…scared," he said slowly.

Dragonboy knew there were lots of
times when someone might feel scared.

When it's very dark.

When it's very loud.

When you're trying
something new.

When you don't
want to let go.

Or when you're just not feeling brave.

"The...shadows...are...so...dark," Simon explained.

"They're dancing!" said Yellow Kitty. "Look how the trees sway."

"A whole new world comes alive at night," Dragonboy said, squeezing his friend's paw.

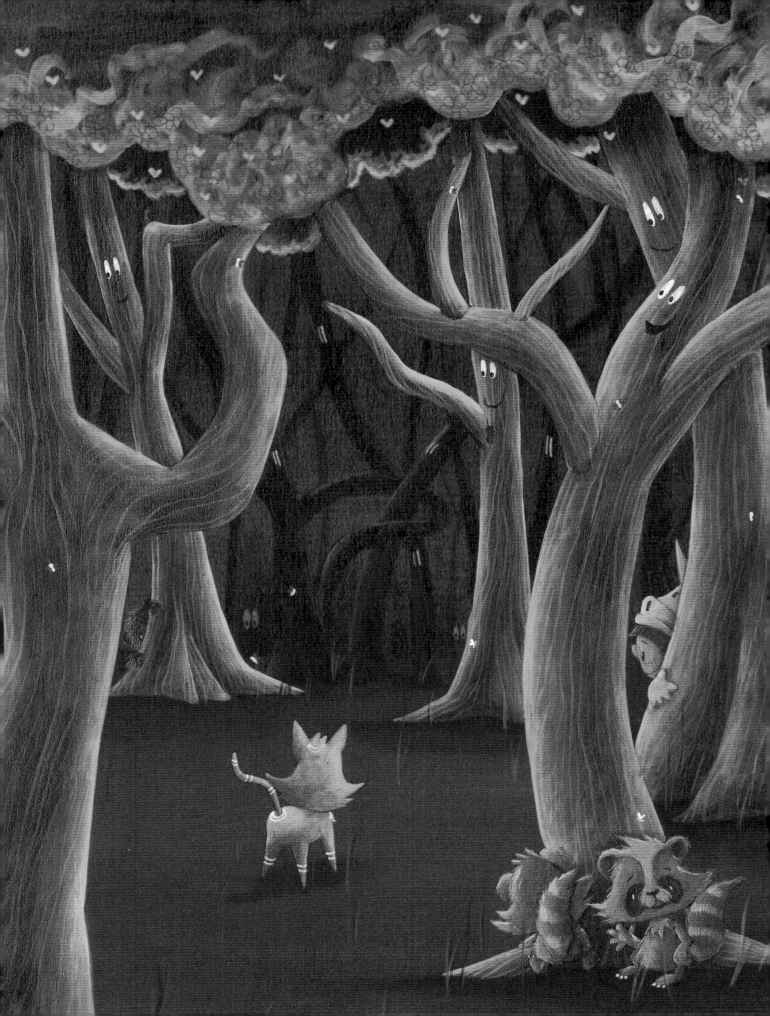

Simon was still stuck in place.

"Try listening instead of looking," Dragonboy suggested.

"I hear crickets chirping," said Darwin.

"I hear myself breathing," said Yellow Kitty.

Then they heard a hooting sound.

"What…was…that?" asked Simon.

"It's an owl," said Drako.
"Look up there!"

"I wonder if it can see the whole night world,"
said Dragonboy.
    (Imagine how much you could see
        perched high in a tree.)

The silence broke with a snap and a crack.

"What...was...THAT?" Simon asked again.

Yellow Kitty peered into the bushes.

"It's three little fox cubs! Let's play with them!"

Darwin wandered to the top of a hill. "Come look at the stars!" he called. "One, two, three…"

"How many can there be?" wondered Drako.

"Enough for each person in the world to have their own special star," said Dragonboy.

"Everyone make a wish!" said Yellow Kitty.
(Always make a wish when someone invites you to.)

Drako was done wishing first and opened his eyes.

"These stars are alive!" he shouted.

"Fireflies," breathed Yellow Kitty.

"One, two, three..." Darwin started a new count.

Simon caught the first firefly.

"That...tickles," he said with a smile—

—until something whooshed past him. "Yikes!"

"Don't worry," Dragonboy said. "It's only Unicorngirl. I think she's been wanting to join us."

"Oh," said Simon. "That's not so scary."
(Most things aren't as scary
as they seem.)

For the rest of the night,
the friends chased
and raced
and counted
and contemplated.

And no one felt scared or left out.

Soon, the stars began to fade.

"It's time to say goodbye," said Dragonboy.

But Unicorngirl didn't want to let her firefly go.

"Look," Dragonboy said. "They like to be together, just like us."

(Everything is better when shared with friends.)

Unicorngirl smiled and nodded, then watched as her firefly flitted away.

"Thank you," Dragonboy said as the friends arrived back home. "You all made my wish come true: a *wonderful* night with you."

"That was my wish, too," blurted out Drako.

"And mine," said Yellow Kitty.

"And mine," said Darwin.

Simon yawned. "Mine…was…to…be…safe…
and…sound…in…bed."
  (That is a very good wish, too.)

Back in the tent,
not too far from you,
at the very edge of the backyard,
Dragonboy snuggled into his sleeping bag.

The night had held all sorts of wonders.

He couldn't wait to see what the day
might bring next.

Dragonboy

Unicorngirl

Simon